ARKFALL

A novella by

CAROLYN IVES GILMAN

PHOENIX   BOOKLETS

an imprint of

Rockville, Maryland

ISBN: 978-1-61242-109-4

www.PhoenixPick.com
Great Science Fiction at Great Prices

Published by Phoenix Pick
an imprint of Arc Manor
P. O. Box 10339
Rockville, MD 20849-0339
www.ArcManor.com

About "Arkfall"

Carolyn Ives Gilman

In my day job as a historian, I read and write a lot about exploration and discovery. Part of the fun of this literature is that we readers can imagine ourselves magically whisked out of our normal routines and obligations, transported to an exotic world where real-life responsibilities do not exist. But when it came to writing a story about exploration, I wanted to think about whether discovery could happen without abdicating the bonds of family and community.

The setting for "Arkfall" evolved from a daisy chain of speculations. I was reading about Europa, a planet-sized moon covered by a global sea that is capped with ice, and I thought (as most people must), "What if there are deep sea rift zones there, as on Earth? Couldn't life evolve there as it did here, based on the heat and minerals from deep-sea vents rather than photosynthesis from sunlight?" This was before we knew about Enceladus, which almost certainly does have volcanic activity under the ice, since it spews out eruptions of water vapor laced with organic compounds.

That first speculation led to: "What would it be like to live in such an environment?" It seemed like life under an ice-capped sea would be claustrophobic and cautious, so I invented the sort of society that would be needed to cope with such an environment. But it also seemed like a failure of imagination to assume that residents of such a world would stick with our mechanistic technologies. So I posited a type of technology that doesn't start with physics, but with biology. Rather than building habitats and ships inspired by the brittle mechanism, this society would invent things modeled on the pliable living cell.

It doesn't make for an exploration story that resembles Lewis and Clark very much—but that's kind of the point.

1. Golconda Station

Normally, the liquid sky over Golconda was oblivion black: no motion, no beacons to clock the passage of time. But at Arkfall the abyss kindled briefly with drifting lights. From a distance, they looked like a rain of photisms, those false lights that swim in darkened eyes. First a mere smudge of light, then a globe, and finally a pockmarked little world floating toward the seafloor station.

The arks were coming home.

From the luminous surface of the ark *Cormorin*, Osaji felt the opacity that had oppressed her for months lifting. All around her, arks floated like wayward thoughts piercing the deep unconsciousness of the sea. The sight was worth having put on the wetsuit and squeezed out to see. She was oblivious to the pressure of the deep water, having been born and bred to it. Even the chill, only a few degrees above freezing, seemed mild to her, warmed by the volcanic exhalations of the Cleft of Golconda on the seafloor below.

After months of drifting through the Saltese Sea, the arkswarm had come for respite to the station of Golconda, the place where their rounds began and ended. Osaji's light-starved eyes, accustomed to seeing only the glowing surface of her own ark and any others that happened to be drifting nearby, savored the sense of space and scale that the glowing domes and refinery lights below her created. There was palpable distance here, an actual landscape.

It would have looked hellish enough to other eyes. A chain of seafloor vents snaked along the valley floor, glowing in places with reddish rock-heat. Downstream, black smokers belched out a filthy brew loaded with minerals from deep under the planet's gravity-tortured crust. Tall chimneys encased the older vents. Everywhere the seafloor was covered with thick, mucky vegetation feeding on the dissolved nutrients: fields of tubeworms, blind white crabs, brine shrimp, clams, eels, seagrass, tiny translucent fish. The carefully nurtured ecosystem had been transported from faraway Earth to this watery planet of Ben. To Osaji, the slimy brown jungle looked like the richest crop, the most fertile field, a welcoming abundance of life. Patient generations had created it.

Beside her, a pore in the lipid membrane of the ark released a jet of bubbles, making the vessel sink slowly toward the floodlit harbor where a dozen other arks already clustered, docked to flexible tube chutes that radiated from the

4

domes like glowing starfish arms. It was time for Osaji to go inside, but still she lingered. All her problems lay inside *Cormorin*'s membrane, neatly packaged. Once she went inside, they would immerse her again.

A voice sputtered over her ear radio, "Will she be coming in soon?" It was the Bennite idiom: tentative, nonconfrontational. But no less coercive for that. Osaji sighed, making her breather mask balloon out, and answered, "She will be pleased to."

Pushing off, she dived downward past the equator of the ark's globe, gliding over its silvery surface. The top portion of the ark was filled with bladders of gas that controlled buoyancy and atmosphere, along with the tanks of bacteria and algae that processed seawater into usable components. Only at the bottom did the humans live, like little mitochondria in their massive host.

On the ark's underbelly Osaji found a pore, tickled its edges till it expanded, then thrust her arms and head in, pulling herself though the soft, clinging lips of the opening. Inside, she shook the water off her short black hair and removed her facemask and fins. She was in a soft-walled, gently glowing tube leading upward to the living quarters. As she walked, her feet bounded back from the rubbery floor.

The quarters seemed brightly lit by the snaking vapor-tubes on the ceiling. As soon as Osaji entered the bustling corridor, Dori's two children crowded around her, asking questions. Their mother peered out the aperture of her room and called to them, "Is it polite to bother her when she has so much packing to do?" The comment was really aimed at Osaji. Dori's family had left her in no doubt that she and her baggage would be leaving the ark at Golconda.

Osaji ran her finger along the sensitive lip of the aperture into her own small rooms, and the membrane retracted to let her through. The first cavity inside, where Osaji had lived for the last round, was stripped bare, all her belongings packed into sacks and duffels. She paused at the aperture to the adjoining vacuole and called out, "Mota?"

"Saji?" came a thin voice from within. Osaji coaxed the membrane open and had to suppress a groan of dismay. Inside, a frail, white-haired woman sat amid a disorganized heap of belongings. She had not packed a thing since Osaji had left her. If anything, she had emptied out some of the duffels already packed.

The old woman's mild face lit up. "Thank goodness you're back! I was getting worried. Where did you go?"

"Outside. I told you I was going outside."

"Did you." She was not contradicting, just commenting. No argument or reproach ever came from Mota. She was the sweetest-tempered aged on the planet. It sometimes drove her granddaughter to distraction.

"Time is short now," Osaji said, seizing a sack and starting to shove clothes in it. "*Cormorin* docks at Golconda in a few minutes."

"I remember Golconda," Mota said reflectively.

"I know you do. You must have been there sixty times."

"Your mother, Manuko, got off there one round and tried going barnacle. She could never get used to it. But your sister—she actually married a barnacle." She said it as if Osaji had never heard the news.

"Yes, we're going to see her in a few minutes."

"Oh, good," Mota said. "That will be nice."

Osaji didn't say: And you are going to stay with her from now on, and set me free.

The gentle jostle of docking came before Osaji was ready. Dori poked her head in the aperture to say, "We've arrived. Everyone can leave now."

Seething inside, Osaji said pleasantly, "In a moment."

Cormorin had not been a happy ark this round. When joining, Osaji had mistaken Dori's conventional expressions of respect for real tolerance of the aged. Once under way, Dori had voiced one sweetly phrased complaint after another, and it had become obvious that she resented Mota's presence. The old lady should not walk the corridors alone, because she might fall. She shouldn't be allowed in the kitchen, because she might put on a burner and forget it. She shouldn't help with the cleaning, because her eyes were too poor to see dirt. Once, Dori had said to Osaji, "Caring for an aged is so much responsibility. I already have as much as I can bear." So she had taken no responsibility at all for Mota. Everything had landed on Osaji, making Dori hint with false sympathy that she wasn't pulling her weight around the ark. Mota had ended the round a virtual prisoner in her room, because just seeing her seemed to give Dori a fresh case of martyrdom.

The corridors of Golconda station were a shock to anyone fresh from floatabout. A floater's world was a yielding womb of liquid where there was never a raised voice, never a command given; floaters all went their lone ways, within the elaborate choreography of their shared mission. The barnacles' world was a gray, industrial place of hard floors, angles, crowds, and noise. Barnacles had to move in coordinated lockstep—cooperative obedience, they called it. They were packed in too close to survive any other way. The two ways of life were the yin and yang of Ben: each needed the other, but neither partook of the other's nature.

A line of porters stood by with electric carts in the hallway, so Osaji approached one, trying to conceal her diffidence. Codes of courtesy were abrupt here, because barnacles always thought time for interaction was short. The porter named an outrageous price. When she attempted to tell her story, he said the Authority set the amount, and there was nothing he could do about it. She gave in, feeling diminished.

Mota's baggage filled the cart, so Osaji gave the porter the address, saw the old lady safely seated beside him, and hefted her own bags to walk, more to avoid dealing with another driver than to save the money. Soon she was feeling jostled and invaded-upon. The corridor was half blocked off by some noisy construction, and the moving crowd was compressed into a narrow chute made dingy with too many passing feet and too much human exhalation. When she emerged into one of the domes, she looked for a spot out of traffic to gaze at the wonder of wide space. The brightly lit geodesic framework spanned a parklike area of greenery ringed with company shops and Authority offices. A grove of trees soared a breathtaking twenty feet over her head. They lifted her heart on their branches: she, too, had the potential to grow lofty. If only she could worm past this stricture in her life, she would be able to reach up again.

And yet, above the trees, the weight of a frigid planetary ocean pressed down. It was a Quixotic gesture of the builders, really, to have nurtured a form of life so unsuited to the environment. Perhaps the human genome was coded for this urge to put things where they didn't belong. Osaji knew floaters who spoke of the trees with hauteur, for they were symbols of in-adaptability. The floaters were the ones who had pioneered a truly Bennite way of life, not this transplanted impossibility of a habitat. Osaji caught her breath in wonder as a bright bird winged overhead.

The impulse to act on her long-laid plans grew strong in her. Why not now, before she saw her family, so it would be an accomplished fact? She knew the proper place to go, for she had sought it out last round, but with-out enough resolve. This time would be different.

¤

The Immigration Authority was a neatly aligned place. The agents sat behind a row of plain desks, and the clients sat in three straight lines of chairs facing them, waiting for their numbers to be called. No one looked at anyone else. The agents' soft voices filled the room with a background of sibilant word-sounds that made no words.

When Osaji's turn came to face an agent, she dropped her bags in an untidy heap on the floor around her chair. She had barely sat down before she blurted out, "Your client wishes to leave the planet."

The agent was a young woman about Osaji's age, but much prettier, wearing a blue uniform with a crisp white collar. Calm and competent, she said, "Why would that be?"

Osaji had not come prepared to answer this question. She swam in a sea of reasons, drowning in them. She was afraid to open her mouth for fear she would choke on them. At last she chose one that seemed least danger-ous. "To see new places."

"So it is a tourism desire?" the young woman asked politely. Her hands were folded on the desktop.

"No." Osaji realized that she had made it sound trivial and self-indulgent. "It is necessary for opportunity. To broaden one's self."

"Education, then?"

Knowing the next question would be which offworld academy had ad-mitted her, Osaji said, "No. It is better to work one's way."

"Financial enrichment?"

"No!" That was antisocial selfishness. "A person needs to learn the ways of the great worlds, to experience different cultures. How else can a person's mind expand? Ben is small and stifling."

Though she had spoken the last words very softly, the agent caught them. Outwardly, the woman did not react, but her questions changed.

"Has the Great Work ceased to inspire?"

"No." Osaji shifted nervously. She still felt the Great Work of creating a habitable planet from this cratered ball of ice was a noble one, and she honored the dedication of the generations who had gotten this far. But it was slow, centuries-slow, and she would not live to see it done. If she did not leave, she would never even see what a habitable planet looked like. "It is just.... We *are* free to leave? They always say so."

The agent smiled, making her even more formidably pretty. "Of course. It is just that clients often think they wish to leave when what they really need is to solve some personal problem. It would be very selfish to ask us to spend the resources to send a person off-planet just because someone cannot face an obligation."

The shame Osaji felt then was like nausea, a sickness rising from her stomach. The woman had seen right through her. Osaji had tried to cloak her cowardice in brave fantasies to make it look less ugly. The truth was, leaving Ben meant abandoning her own grandmother, that sweet and helpless aged who had raised her and who now chained her with responsibility she didn't want. It was so low, Osaji sat staring at her hands folded in her lap, unable to raise her eyes. And yet, losing her hope of escape felt so painful she couldn't move from the chair, couldn't let some other more deserving person take her place.

The agent said gently, "Very few people who leave Ben like it on other worlds. We are not suited for that sort of life. Besides, it is nobler to face things here than to flee."

Osaji made no sound, but prickly tears began to brim over and drip on her clasped hands. She tried to think as a noble person ought to, about bravely facing her problems, but instead she felt a black resentment. Mota would live for many years yet. Her body did not make her old; her straying mind was the problem. The disease had come upon her early—so early that Osaji, the last grandchild, did not yet have a life of her own, and so became the family solution. The true tragedy was Mota's. But being her caretaker, there was nothing to aim for—no goal, only monotonous endurance until the end. And then what? All Osaji's chances would be gone by then.

At that lowest point, when her prison seemed impenetrable, she was distracted in the most irritating way, by a raised voice at the desk next to her. A wiry, weatherbeaten foreigner was berating his agent.

"Are you going to get your prigging rear in gear, or do I have to raise hell?"

The man's agent, a timid young woman who looked acutely embarrassed by the attention he was drawing, tried to calm him in a low tone.

"Don't you whisper at me, you simpering little bureaucrat," he said even louder. "You are going to give me a visa and a ticket on the first shuttle out of this clam steamer, or you are going to hear some real decibels."

"Please, sir," she pleaded. "Shouting at your agent will not solve your problem."

"You don't know what a problem is, sister. At this rate, you're going to know pretty soon."

Osaji's agent went to the rescue of her traumatized colleague. "What seems to be the issue?"

The unkempt offworlder turned on her. He was only half-shaved, and wore mercenary coveralls. "The *issue*, my dear, is this whole lickspittle planet—on which vertebrate life does not yet exist. The entire goddamned culture is based on passive aggression. Don't you all know this is a *frontier*? Where's your initiative, your self-reliance? Where are your new horizons? I've never seen such an insular, myopic, conformist, small-minded bunch of people in my life. This planet is a small town preserved in formaldehyde. Get me *out* of here!"

Osaji had often thought the same things about Ben, but hearing them expressed so coarsely made her bristle. The intensity of the emotions she had been feeling reversed polarity, turning outward at the hateful offworlder beside her. He had had chances she would never get, and what had he done with them?

A manager came out from one of the back offices and tried to draw the man into a private room to pacify him. The offworlder, perhaps sensing he would lose his audience, stood up to defend his ground. He was short and his spindly legs were a little bowed, but he had a ferocious demeanor.

"Do you know who you're talking to, son?" he said. "Ever hear of Scrappin' Jack Halliday, who captured Plamona Outpost in the War of the Wrist?" When no one around him showed the slightest recognition, he gave an oath. "Of course not. You bottom-dwellers don't care about anything unless it happens ten feet in front of your noses."

The manager tried to be conciliatory, but Osaji could see it would have no effect. Her anger had been burning like a slow fuse all last round, and now it reached the end. She stood up and shouted, "Did you come here just to make us listen to your profanity and your complaints? If you can't make it on Ben, that's too bad—but stop whining!"

Scrappin' Jack looked like he had been ambushed from the direction he least expected. Rattled, he stared at Osaji as if hearing phantom sniper fire, and all he said was, "What the—?"

A little appalled at what she had done, Osaji sat down again facing her agent. At last the manager was able to lead the intemperate offworlder away. The office slowly resumed its normal functioning.

"That's what they're all like on the other worlds," Osaji's agent said in a low voice. "An emigrant has to cope with that, day in and day out. Are you sure—?"

"No," Osaji said. "I think the lifestream put him there to show me something. I am not supposed to leave Ben."

The agent smiled encouragingly.

"I am grateful for your good work." Outwardly composed again, Osaji gathered up her bags and left, feeling wrung out but relieved.

2. Barnacles and Floaters

Osaji's sister Kitani lived with her family in a dome that was divided up into pie-shaped Domestic Units surrounding a central dining and recreation area. Kitti's DU was on the second floor, meaning it was smaller, though the family had been on the waiting list for an upgrade for two rounds. It was one of the compromises people made to live barnacle. Brother-in-law Juko answered the door with a red-faced, howling baby in his arms. He was a gangling man with a perpetual, slightly goofy smile—and it was just as well, for the hubbub he ushered her into would have induced hypertension in anyone less tuned out. The DU had only two rooms—a sleeproom and an everything-else room—and their older daughter was having a tantrum in the sleeproom. The main room was simply crammed with furniture, cookware, baby strollers, clothes, and diaper bins. Mota's baggage formed an obstacle in the middle of the floor. "Tell your Aunt Saji it is good to see her," Juko shouted to the baby in his arms. As an in-law, it wasn't polite for him to speak to Osaji directly.

Osaji dumped her bags on the floor—there was nowhere else to put them—and tried to give Juko a greeting just as the baby threw up all down his front. He smiled as if his face didn't know what else to do, and disappeared into the sleeproom.

Osaji's grandmother sat in an armchair, looking slightly dazed. Kitti came out of the sleeproom and gave Osaji a frazzled hug. Looking at the mound of baggage, she said, "Is it that you're changing arks?"

"Yes," Osaji said. "It wasn't a good fit, with *Cormorin*." Propriety forbade her to come any closer to speaking ill of others.

"That's too bad," Kitti said with a remote, distracted sympathy, as if it didn't concern her. Osaji wanted to pull her aside right then and make her plea, but it didn't seem like the right moment.

The right moment didn't come that evening, either—a crowded, chaotic succession of rearrangements, feedings, and infant outbursts. Not until the next morning did Osaji and Kitti get some time alone together, when they took the children to the playground in an adjoining dome. They sat on a bench and watched barnacle children frolic under the overhanging sea.

Kitti was first to bring up the subject. "Mota's really deteriorated," she said. The bald declaration—not tentative, not a question—showed how shocked she had been. It made Osaji uncomfortable.

"You think so?" she said, though it was exactly what she had wanted to talk about.

"Don't you? She's much more weak and unsteady on her feet. You ought to get her more exercise. You know, ageds can still build up muscle tone if they work at it."

"Ah," Osaji said.

"And her mind seems to be wandering. She repeats herself, and loses track of what people are saying. You need to stimulate her more, challenge her mentally, get her involved."

"Isn't it just that she is old?" Osaji said.

Kitti mistook it for a real question. "Age doesn't have to mean deterioration. There are plenty of aged who are still intelligent and active."

"But Mota's not."

"No, she needs to be encouraged to improve herself."

Osaji felt an upwelling of desperation. "I've been wondering whether an ark is the best setting for her. Perhaps she would be better off elsewhere."

"Where?" Kitti said. "The domes for the aged are overcrowded, and you can't get anyone in without a medical permit. She's not that badly off."

"Still, it's really hard in an ark. There's no room for unproductives in an ark. And it's not just her; she makes me an unproductive too, because I have to look after her. It's two wasted berths, not just one." And two wasted lives.

Abruptly, Kitti changed the subject. "What about you? Have you met anyone?"

Osaji thought back on the slow torture of the last round: every day regimented by the need to look after Mota punctually. Not once had she broken free from that elastic band of obligation. Not for one moment had Mota been completely out of her mind. There had been no space left for anything else.

"You could register, you know," Kitti said. "The computers do a good job matching people."

Most Bennites found mates this way. In a place where everyone lived in isolated pockets scattered about the seafloor, it was the most practical way to meet someone compatible. Osaji had resisted it for years, out of a waning hope that she would meet someone the old, magical way, guided by the fateful currents of the lifestream. At the thought of her naiveté, she felt a sharp ache of disappointment. "Who would take a mate with an aged attached?" she said, and the bitterness sounded in her voice.

Kitti finally heard it. "You can't let her ruin your life," she said.

Though Kitti had not meant to sound accusatory, Osaji felt it that way. She burst out, "Kitti, if you would only take her for a round…"

"Me?" Kitti said in astonishment. "I have the young ones. You've seen our DU."

"I know." But the young ones, the DU—they were all Kitti's choices. Osaji had had no choices of her own. Kitti's had foreclosed all of hers.

The feeling of constriction returned. The thought of another round like the last was unendurable.

"I'm afraid," Osaji said in a low voice, "that I'm going to start to hate her."

Warmly, Kitti put an arm around Osaji's shoulder and hugged her tight. "Oh, you would never do that. You're a good and loving granddaughter. What you do for her is really admirable." She looked in Osaji's bleak face and said coaxingly, "Come on, smile. I know you love her, and that's what counts."

Kitti had gotten so used to dealing with children that she couldn't interact any other way. All problems seemed like childhood problems to her, all solutions reduced to lollipops and lullabies. Osaji stood abruptly, wanting to do something evil, wanting to do anything but what a good and loving granddaughter would do.

That evening, after dinner, she rose and said, "It is necessary to go on an errand." Luckily, Kitti and Juko were busy with the children, and no one offered to go with her.

The docks were still crowded with delivery carts, baggage handlers, and floaters coming and going. She walked down the harshly lit aisle, pausing at each tubular port where arkmates had posted their crew needs. She hurried past *Cormorin*'s port, noting resentfully that they were advertising two berths.

While she was reading a posting for a hydroponics technician, wondering if she could pass, a too-familiar voice made her whirl around and look. There he was—the outworlder, Scrappin' Jack, trying to impress a circle of young longshoremen. She could hardly believe the authorities had not gotten rid of him. As her eyes fell on him, he looked up and saw her. "Holy crap," he said, "it's the shrew."

Quickly she looked away to avoid any further contact, but he was not so easily discouraged. Pushing through the traffic, he came to her side. He was barely taller than she, a compressed packet of offensiveness. "Listen," he said, "about yesterday, in that office—you've got to understand, I was tripped out on cocaine."

As if that were an excuse. She scowled. "Why would an outworld mercenary come here?"

He gave a dry, rasping laugh. "Sister, you're not the first to ask. They asked me all through those godawful treatments for high-pressure adaptation. But rumor was, there were empty spaces here, unexplored territory, room to spread out. All true—it's just under tons of water, and the habitations are a bit too togetherly for me."

An idea occurred to her, brilliant in its spitefulness. "Has he considered going on floatabout? That is the way to explore Ben." To spend months trapped in a bubble drifting through opaque blackness, that was the real Ben. It would drive the man mad.

"You think so?" he said.

"Yes," she said encouragingly. "There is an ark looking for new crew. It's named *Cormorin*, just down the hall there. An applicant should ask for Dori."

He looked like he was actually considering it. "Why not?" he said. "It couldn't get worse. Thanks, kiddo."

As he was turning to go, the floor shifted slightly underfoot, and the hanging lamps swayed. He stumbled. "Whoa," he said, "I thought I was sober." Osaji didn't bother to tell him it had been a ground tremor, all too common here along the cleft. She turned to escape the other way.

Across the hall, at the mouth to the next port, a tall, lean woman with a patch over one eye was watching, cross-armed. As Osaji passed, she said, "Is someone looking for an opening?"

Osaji stopped. The woman's shaggy hair was gray-streaked, but she looked fit, with a composed, cool look of self-sufficiency about her. The eye patch seemed like an affectation, a declaration of nonconformity, and Osaji suddenly decided she liked it.

"Lura of *Divernon*," the woman introduced herself.

"Osaji of ... nowhere, right now."

"*Divernon* needs a hand to help out at odd jobs, particularly wet ones."

Osaji looked down. "Your applicant enjoys wet." She could not say she was good at it—that would seem unhumble—but she was. "Her profile is listed in the registry."

"I don't need to see her profile," Lura said. "I just saw her handle that offworld jerk."

Osaji looked up, astonished that anyone would commit to a crewmate without studying their compatibility profile. Lura's one eye was disconcertingly alert, but laughing. From her face, it looked like she often laughed.

"Does the young adventurer come with anyone else?" she asked.

Osaji blushed, feeling a pang, but said, "No."

"It would not matter if they were less than married." Lura had mistaken the cause of the blush.

"How many does *Divernon* hold?" Osaji asked, to change the subject.

"Myself, Mikita—and you. We were hoping to get a couple to join us, but we can't wait any longer. The Authority wants us to vacate this port tonight."

"Just three?" It was a skeleton crew. They would work hard, but enjoy a lot of privacy.

"*Divernon*'s last crew got married and left us," Lura said wryly. "Maybe a single will be safer."

That sounded like a happy ark, if a little lonely. But just now, lonely seemed good. "The ark leaves tonight?" she said.

"Can Osaji of nowhere be ready?"

"Yes. She needs to fetch her baggage."

"Fetch away," Lura said.

As Osaji hailed an electric cart, she could scarcely believe what she was doing. Joining an ark on impulse, without studying the others' profiles, without even meeting one of the two she would spend the next round with. It was an act of lunacy, or desperation.

When she got back to Kitti's DU, she had the cart driver wait out of sight while she went in, hoping to find the others preparing for bed so she could slip out unseen. Juko was in the sleeproom putting the children to bed, but Kitti was still in the front with Mota. She had opened up Mota's baggage and was sorting through it. One wastebasket was already overflowing with items she had decided to discard.

"What are you doing?" Osaji said.

"Getting rid of some of the useless junk she is hauling around," Kitti said with efficient cheerfulness. "Really, Saji, haven't you looked through these bags? Some of this stuff must be fifty years old." She held up a battered wooden flute, missing its reed. "What's this for?"

It was the flute Great-uncle Yamada had played on the day they married the two arks, *Steptoe* and *Elderon*, when Mota was young. Osaji had heard the story so many times she had often thought she would scream before hearing it again. She looked to Mota, expecting her to start the tale, but the old lady was withdrawn and silent.

"Do you play it?" Kitti asked pointedly. Mota shook her head. "Then what use is it? Why carry it around?"

"Do whatever you want with it," Mota said, looking away. "I don't mind." Kitti stuffed it in the trash bin.

Osaji looked at the discards. There was the dirty plush toy their grandfather had given Mota when she first got pregnant, the rock Yamada had brought from the surface, the little shell pendant for luck. Osaji knew all the stories. "Kitti, these things are hers. You can't just throw them out."

"I'm asking her," Kitti said. "She agrees."

Osaji could see it now: Mota was going to become an improvement project for Kitti. And Mota would just acquiesce, as she always had done. She had spent so many years trying to please others, she didn't even remember what it was like to want something for herself. A tweak of compassion made Osaji say, "Can I talk to her, Kitti?"

Kitti climbed to her feet. "I've got to go check on the little ones."

Osaji sat down next to Mota. The old woman took her hand and squeezed it, but said nothing.

"Mota, I need to know something," Osaji said softly. "Do you want to come with me for another round on an ark, or would you rather stay here?"

Mota said nothing. Osaji waited, then said, "You have to decide. I'm leaving tonight."

"I want whatever you want," Mota said. "Whatever makes you happy."

Even though she had half known that would be the answer, Osaji still felt a familiar burn of frustration. Her grandmother's passivity was a kind of manipulation: a way to put all the responsibility onto others, an abdication of adulthood. Mota had always been like this, and there was absolutely no way to fight it. It made everyone around her into petty dictators. Osaji hated the role, and she hated Mota for forcing her into it.

It should have been a decision made in love, but instead it was grim duty in Osaji's heart when she said, "All right. You're coming with me."

She emptied out the wastebasket and stuffed all the things back into the bag they had come from, then hefted as many duffels as she could carry and took them down to the waiting cart. The baggage took three trips, and on the fourth she helped Mota to the door. It crossed her mind to leave without saying anything, but at the last moment she stuck her head in the sleeproom door. "Kitti, we're going now. Our ark is leaving."

"Now?" Kitti sounded startled, but not unhappy at the news. She got up to hug them both, wish them a happy round, and to press some food on them, which Osaji declined.

All the way to the docks Osaji rehearsed what to say to her new arkmates. But when they got to *Divernon*, there was no sign of Lura, or anyone else. She helped Mota through the flexible tube into the ark, calling out "Hello? *Divernons?*" There was no answer.

Finding the spare quarters was easy, so she left Mota inside and went back to ferry in the baggage. It occurred to her that it would be easy to hide Mota's presence till they had embarked, and then it would be too late for anyone to object.

She had just hooked the last bag over her shoulder and paid the driver when a shout from down the hall made her freeze. "Hey, shrike!"

It was Scrappin' Jack, coming down the hall like a torpedo locked on her coordinates. She would have ducked inside the ark, but feared he would just follow her.

From twenty feet away he bellowed, "What's the idea, sending me to that shrink-wrapped prig?"

Everyone in earshot was staring, and Osaji could feel her ears glow. "A man should be quiet," she pleaded.

"You thought you could pull a fast one on Scrappin' Jack, did you? Well, news flash: it takes more balls than you've got to screw me over." He waved a hand as if to clear away invisible gnats. "That didn't come out right."

"Go away!" Osaji commanded. Down the hall, Lura was approaching with another woman at her side. Keenly aware of first impressions, Osaji tried to pretend that the raging eruption in front of her did not exist. She waved at them cheerfully.

With a deafening crash, the floor jerked sideways, flinging everyone to the ground. Carts overturned, their contents scattered, and broken glass rained down. Again the floor bucked, sending Osaji skidding across tile into a wall with bruising force. For a moment there was silence, except for the groan of stressed girders and the ominous sound of falling water. A stream of it was running down the floor. Then a third jolt came. Osaji scrabbled for a handhold.

"Quick, into the ark!" said a voice, and Lura's strong hand was pulling her up. Osaji was lying across the entry, blocking the way into the ark. Not trusting her balance, she scrambled on hands and knees up the chute. When she got into the ark, it was bobbing around in the turbulent water like a balloon on a string. Barely able to keep upright, she turned to help Lura through— and found it was not Lura behind her after all. It was the spacer, Jack.

"What is the awful man doing here?" Osaji cried.

He looked as buffeted as she. "Some pirate dyke shoved me in the umbilical and told me to climb. I climbed."

"Where is she?"

At that moment the room turned sideways and they were thrown in a heap onto the yielding wall. The aperture connecting them to the mooring tube contracted and disappeared. That meant they had broken free of the tube; but still the ark wasn't rising. Instead of floating in the smooth motion of the sea, *Divernon* was jerking like a leashed animal.

"There's still a mooring line attached," Osaji said. She snatched up the breather and face mask that had been knocked from their pocket on the wall. "I'm going to find Lura. You, stay here."

There was no time to put on a suit, so she just stripped to her underwear, strapped on the mask, and thrust head-first through the lips of the orifice. Only a few bubbles of air escaped with her.

The first shock was the temperature of the water—bathtub warm. The second was the noise—a mere growl inside, here it was like the roar of a thousand engines. The water was nearly opaque, full of roiled-up sediment. The harbor lights were still on, turning everything into a golden brown fog. Feeling her way along the surface of the ark, she searched blindly for the line that was tying them down, for it would lead to the station.

It was taut when she found it; the ark was tugging on it like a creature mad to escape. By feel, she traced it down to a clip attached to a U-bolt on the dock. Now she realized what must have happened; the other two lines had broken, detaching the ark from the landing tube before Lura and her companion could get in. Now Osaji only had to find the tube in this blinding muck.

Before she could move, she felt the metal under her foot bowing out. The last U-bolt was giving way. She clutched the line tight as if she could pull the ark down, and keep it tethered.

There was a metallic pop and the bolt came loose. With Osaji still clinging to the line, the ark rose swiftly into the upwelling water. Instinctively she hung on as water raced past her ears.

They quickly cleared the turbid layer, and Osaji saw what lay below. The Cleft of Golconda was erupting. A raging glow of blood-red lava snaked along the seafloor, obscured by hellish clouds of steam. As she looked down on the station, another tremor passed through it, and a panel on the largest dome collapsed. In seconds, the adjacent panels were caving inward, the dome crumpling. A huge bubble of air escaped, and all the lights went out except the livid lava.

The ark was caught in a steam-propelled plume of hot water, flying upward. Darkness closed in. Osaji could no longer see the cleft below, nor the line above; the only light in the world was the dim bioluminescent globe of *Divernon*. Her hands were turning numb. She forced them to clamp down on the line. If she let go, she was lost.

Her ears began to pop. They were rising too fast; the pressure was dropping dangerously. She needed to get inside quickly. Setting her teeth, she tried to climb the line, hand over hand; but she was pulling against the rushing water, and didn't have the strength.

Then she felt a tug on the line, and her spirits revived. She kicked to draw closer. Pain shot through her legs. *Get me in!* she prayed.

The skin of *Divernon* was stretched taut, she saw as she came closer to it. If the ark kept on rising, it would pop like an overfilled balloon, unless someone inside vented gas. Slowly, too slowly, the distance between her and the ark's skin lessened. At last she could reach up and grasp the edge of the hole where the line disappeared inside. But when it began to open to admit her, the pressurized gas inside came shooting out in a jet, sending the ark spinning and wrapping the line around it. Osaji's body thumped against the surface hard enough to knock the breath out of her. But it was just what she needed. She let go of the line and it snaked away into darkness while she clung to the tacky surface of the ark. It felt reassuringly familiar. Slowly, muscles cramping, she crept along till she got to the orifice, and dived inside.

Someone was swearing. It sounded like, "Bull banging damn!"

The ark was still spinning; Osaji was thrown forward on top of Scrappin' Jack as the wall turned into the floor, then into a wall again. As the rotation slowed, they came to rest a few feet apart, staring at each other.

"What the gutting hell are you doing alive?" he said, holding up the empty end of the line. When she had let go, he must have thought her lost.

"Such concern is touching," she said sourly. Ignoring the shooting pains in her arms, she started barefoot up the rubbery organic tube toward the control pod. Jack followed close on her heels.

The control pod of *Divernon* was more elaborately equipped than any she had seen. Arrayed around a curving console, four screens lit the darkened room in eerie colors. Things tumbled about in the spin still littered the floor.

Osaji had been in control pods many times, but had never navigated. Gingerly, she sat down in the swiveling seat, staring at the screens to figure out the ark's status. Jack peered over her shoulder, muttering.

"Sonar, temperatures … what the hell is that?" He pointed at a screen with an animated 3-D diagram.

Osaji was looking at that one, too. "Currents," she said, then pointed to a tiny red point. "That is us."

It showed their true peril. All around them, angry pillars of heated water rose, a forest of deadly plumes, dwarfing them.

Osaji looked for the pressure ratio, and exclaimed, "May the lifestream preserve us!" The pressure inside was enough to burst the ark. "We've got to vent gas, now, or we'll explode."

But her hand hung motionless over the control, for the choice of where to vent was critical. The jet of released air would propel them in the opposite direction, and if they floated into one of those hot plumes, that would be the end. She searched desperately for a safe choice. There was none.

"What are you waiting for?" Jack said.

"I can't decide.…"

"Just do it! Do you want to die?"

Still she hesitated, searching for a solution.

With an oath, Jack reached over her shoulder and slammed his palm down on the control himself.

"You evil, reckless man!" Osaji cried out. "You have killed us."

"You're the one who'll kill us, with your anal dithering," Jack yelled back.

The pressure dropped into a safer range, but just as Osaji had feared, they were slowly floating toward one of the hot upwellings.

Desperately she vented more air to stop their motion. But the plumes on the screen were shifting, converging, leaving *Divernon* no space. Again she vented as a plume seemed to reach out toward them. But it only sent them into the arms of another.

She sat back resignedly. "It is our fate."

"What is?" Jack demanded. He had no idea what was going on.

She didn't answer. She could feel *Divernon* shudder, then rock, as the swift current took it. They were rising again, like a bubble in boiling water, little bumps and shifts betraying their speed. Osaji wanted to look away, but couldn't take her eyes from the screen. Even as she watched, the heat was probably killing the bioengineered outer surface of the craft, the membrane on which their lives depended. It did not matter; they would die anyway, in the terrible heights where no human or habitation was meant to be.

3. Through the Gap

The sonar screen was showing something strange. To their west was a solid return, something gigantic. Osaji increased the range, and felt a flutter of terror in her belly. It was a wall, a sheer cliff towering over them. There was only one thing it could be: the underwater mountain range that rimmed the ancient basin where life had taken such a precarious hold. Improbably, it seemed to curve outward over them like a mouth about to bite down. Osaji stared at the screen for several seconds before she realized what it showed. "Save us!" she exclaimed.

"What?" Jack asked.

"It is showing the bottom of the ice."

All her life it had been a rumor—the unseen cap on the sky, the lightless place where the world turned solid and all life stopped. She could feel it now, hanging above her, miles thick, heavy enough to crush them. She swallowed to quell a claustrophobic flutter in her chest. "The light shuns what is not meant to be looked on," she quoted a saying of the paracletes. Legend said that the underside of the ice was studded with the frozen corpses of people who had died without proper burial, and had floated up.

"I don't understand your problem," Jack said. He pointed to the screen. "The upwellings aren't as bad along the mountain range. Can't you just steer over there?"

Osaji closed her eyes and shook her head at his ignorance. "Our visitor thinks like a spacer," she said.

"So?"

"Arks are not ships. We have no propulsion system."

Jack looked thunderstruck. "You mean you can't control this thing?"

"We can rise and fall. In an emergency, we can vent air from the sides. But we go where the currents take us."

"What if there's no current that happens to be going where you want?"

"Now the visitor understands our problem."

As they rose toward the cap on the world, the screen showing the currents above them changed. Where the upwellings hit the bottom of the ice, there was a region of turbulent eddies and horizontal flows.

Jack was fidgeting nervously. "What happens when we hit that?"

"We will go where the lifestream takes us."

"If the lifestream means to feed me to the crabs, I'm swimming against the current."

"On Ben, feeding crabs is a noble calling," Osaji answered. One was supposed to feel serene about it. "It is all part of the Great Work of seeding the ocean with life."

"No offense to Ben," said Jack darkly, "but a body donation wasn't in my plans."

How little anyone's plans counted now! Osaji stood up, saying, "I have to go check on something."

"You're leaving?" he said incredulously. "Now?"

"I need to see if my grandmother is all right."

"You've got an old lady in the ship?"

"Yes. She is not in good health. It would be good for someone to watch the screens while I am gone."

She sprinted down the springy corridor to the quarters where she had left Mota. The room was tumbled and chaotic from the ark's gymnastics. Mota was sitting on the bed, unharmed but confused and disoriented. "Saji, where am I?" she asked.

"Don't worry, Mota," Osaji said. She was about to explain the situation—the eruption, the heat plumes, their danger—when she saw that what Mota really wanted was much simpler. "We're in an ark called *Divernon*. This is your room. Don't unpack yet. I'll come back as soon as I can."

"This is my room?" Mota said, looking around fearfully.

"Yes. Think about how you want to fix it up."

"What ark are we in?"

With a shrinking feeling Osaji repeated, "*Divernon*."

"Aren't we going to Golconda?"

"We just came from Golconda. It—"The last sight of the station flashed vividly before her, cutting off her voice. She didn't want to say what she feared; she didn't even want to think it. Kitti and Juko, the trees, the playground where they had talked—all dark, all cold, all drowned.... She forced it out of her mind. If she thought about it, it might come true.

"Your sister lives there," Mota said. "I don't know how people can live that way, so crowded."

"Well, you don't have to worry about it," Osaji said. She caught Mota's hand and pressed it between hers, longing for the days when she was the child and Mota the one who took care of things. "Mota, I love you," she said. "I wish I could keep you safe."

She left wondering which would have been the more terrible error: dragging Mota along, or leaving her behind.

When she got back to the control pod, the displays had changed. While she had been gone, *Divernon* had hit the turbulent zone, and now a horizontal current was sweeping them swiftly westward, toward the rock wall.

It looked like they were going to smash into it. Osaji stood next to the chair Jack was occupying, to indicate she wanted to sit down in it, but he was mesmerized by the screens and didn't notice her body language. She cleared her throat. "I might be able to keep us alive a little longer," she said.

"How?" he said.

Courtesy was wasted on him, so she said, "If you would allow me to sit...."

At last he got the message and let her have the chair.

The cliff was approaching at an alarming rate. Osaji vented air on their forward side to brake their speed, but they still felt the jar when *Divernon* hit, even inside all the cushioning internal organs. Osaji winced for the poor tortured membrane.

They caromed off the cliff and back into the current, spinning like a top. Now the sonar showed cliffs on every side of them. It took Osaji several seconds to realize they had been swept into a narrow cleft in the rim rock. For several minutes she kept busy sending out strategic jets of air to keep them from crashing into the rocks again.

"Is it safe to be venting so much air?" Jack asked.

It was his spacer instincts talking again. Preoccupied, Osaji said, "Oxygen is a waste product of the membrane cells' metabolism. We are constantly having to get rid of it."

At last the turbulence eased and the cliffs drew back, but the current was still swift. Osaji glanced at the compass to see where they were headed. Then she looked again, for what it showed was impossible.

"That can't be," she said.

"What?"

"We're still going west. But the mountains are behind us."

Ahead, the sonar showed a rugged plain sloping downward. Every moment the current was carrying them farther into it. "We have been swept through a gap in the mountains," Osaji said. Her lips felt numb around the words.

"Is that bad?" Jack said.

"There is only one inhabited region on Ben. The Saltese Sea, behind us, beyond the mountains. We are going into the uninhabited waste."

There was a short silence as Jack absorbed this information. "What's in the uninhabited waste?" he said at last.

"Rocks, water, darkness. No life." No seafloor stations, no other arks, no human voices. For the next round, perhaps for every round after that, until their ark died.

"Send out a distress call," Jack said.

Osaji reached for the low-frequency radio, and spoke into it. "This is the ark *Divernon*. Can anybody hear me?" They waited. Only the hiss of an empty channel came back. Osaji spoke again. "This is *Divernon*. We have been swept through the mountains on the edge of the Saltese Sea. If you can hear us, please answer."

Only silence.

The empty hiss grew oppressive; Osaji switched it off.

"There's got to be something we can do," Jack said.

Trying to sound calm, Osaji said, "If the ark is not too badly damaged, it should recover. It is a self-sustaining system; it can live for many rounds."

"You're telling me this is it," he said. "I'm trapped till I die. In a god-damned underwater balloon along with an invalid and a harpy."

Osaji gave the grimmest smile in the world. "The outworlder is the lucky one," she said. "We are the ones trapped with him."

4. The Wasteland

Three days later, Jack was still rebelling against their situation. He was a bundle of restless energy. While Osaji unpacked and arranged her quarters comfortably for herself and Mota, he prowled the ark, reading the manuals, trying to find a solution. At first she ignored him; but soon the time came to talk about dividing up the essential tasks of keeping an ark running. Osaji drew up a task wheel and brought it into the kitchen to negotiate the division of labor. It was a familiar routine to her, usually done on the third day of round.

But the daunting list of jobs made not a dimple in his monomania. All he wanted to talk about was another of his endless schemes.

"It's not like you don't have engine fuel," Jack said. "You've got a bagful of waste hydrogen up there."

"The hydrogen's not waste," Osaji said. "It is for our fuel cells, to make electricity."

"Then why not rig an electric motor to some propellers?"

"Does someone here know how to make an engine and propellers?"

He gave off a flare of indignation. "I'm not a bleeding mechanic. But damn it, I'd try. It's better than rolling over and taking whatever the lifestream sends you."

"It is antisocial to make one's personal problems into everyone's problems," Osaji said.

"Thank you, Miss Priss," Jack said acidly. He paced up and down before the kitchen table, two steps one way, two steps back. He was constantly in motion like that. It was like having a trapped animal in your home. "What possessed you Bennites to invent a vehicle without any controls?"

"An ark isn't a way of getting someplace," Osaji explained. "It is a place in itself."

He looked ready to ignite, a small two-legged bag of hydrogen himself. "Thanks, but *I* want to steer the place I'm in. This 'wherever you go, there you are' crap is why you've spent two centuries in the Saltese Sea without ever once having poked your noses out to see the rest of Ben. Wasn't anyone curious? No, you're content in your little bubbles. You've got an entire culture of agoraphobes."

Irritated at his refusal to focus on the practical demands of their situation, Osaji set a pair of flippers and breather down on the table in front of him. "Here. Anyone who doesn't wish to be here can swim back."

"Go to hell."

Osaji had had enough of him. She took back the swim gear, and said, "All right, I am going out."

"Out? What do you mean?" He followed her into the corridor.

"Someone has to check the membrane. I should have done it before."

"Isn't that dangerous?"

"Yes." She stopped and turned to him. "It will be a shame if you are left without someone to abuse. Now let me go."

Above the living quarters, the enormous bladders for air, fuel, and ballast water were swollen, shadowy shapes in the dim glow of the outer membrane. Taking a handful of the tough, fibrous white roots that grew on the inside of the globe surface, Osaji hoisted herself up the outer wall. The roots were wet, and soon her hands and feet were glowing white, covered with luminescent bacteria. The smell was fresh and invigorating, for the air here was rich with oxygen. When she had been a child, it had been a favorite game to climb the globe wall and then throw herself down onto the pillowy bladders below. Then, she had not appreciated the consequences of accidentally puncturing one of the membranes.

She had come this way because, despite her bravado in front of Jack, she was afraid to go out. The main orifice to the outside was at the bottom of the ark, and normally she would have used it. But there were emergency entry pores scattered throughout, and one of them was close to the part of the membrane she most needed to inspect.

It was odd; she had never been afraid of the outside before. In fact, she had relished escaping from the close confines of the ark, and always volunteered for wet work. But back home in the Saltese Sea, she had known exactly what lay outside. All the landmarks were mapped, the waters familiar. Here, her rational mind knew from the sensors that nothing was different, but the animal-instinct part of her brain didn't care.

She squeezed out the aperture like a slippery melon seed, into the embrace of cold and silence. At first she clung with her back to the tacky surface of the ark, peering into the water. The dark had a different quality here. In the Saltese Sea, you always knew that light and life hovered just beyond the edge of sight. Here, the dark was absolute ruler. Their ark was a mote in an emptiness the size of continents.

She unhooked the battery-powered searchlight from her belt. For a moment before turning it on, she had to steel herself, not quite knowing what she feared. When at last she shone it out into the water, it revealed nothing. Or, rather, only one thing: the water was extraordinarily clear. No suspended sediments lit the beam, since this was lifeless water. She aimed it up next, out of irrational fear that ice would be hanging over them, but again the beam disappeared. At last she shone it down. Nothing was visible. A hundred meters below them lay the rugged seafloor terrain of pillow lavas and tumbled boulders, but the beam did not reach so far.

Relieved, she pushed away from the ark to scan its surface. It was easy to see where *Divernon* had collided with the cliff, since a patch had been scraped clean of the luminous bacteria that made the rest of the craft glow white. She swam in close to run her hand across the surface, smoothing new bacteria onto the injured spot so it would heal. Then she slowly skimmed the circumference of the sphere, checking for scorches and barren spots, till she came to rest on the top, looking out on her world.

In its way, *Divernon* was alive, like a giant cell: a lipid membrane full of organelles designed to feed on the dissolved salts and carbon dioxide of the sea, and process them into amino acids and hydrocarbons to release again. It was part of the metabolic chain that would slowly, over the centuries, turn Ben's sea into a living ocean. The ark was a giant fertilizer, a life-creator, an indispensable part of the Great Work. But out here there was no Great Work. Isolated from its fellows, *Divernon* was a lost soul.

Why *had* no ark ever ventured out here before? Now that her irritation had washed away, the thought flowed into her that Jack was right. For so many generations Bennites had been content to pursue their rounds, following the currents in an ever-renewing cycle. They had never pushed beyond the boundaries of the familiar, out into the places without names.

Suddenly, Osaji ached with homesickness for the familiar floatabout cycle. If they had left Golconda as usual, just now they would be coming to the Swirl, a spot where the great current eddied, bringing many arks together. It was always a festive time; people visited from ark to ark, exchanging gifts and sometimes moving to find more compatible crewmates. The arks were gaily decorated, full of music, and there was lighthearted romance and water dancing.

The cold began to seep into her joints, so she kicked off to view the ark from below. As she dove down along the flank of the great globe, the feeling of something looming in the blackness behind her grew, so when she reached bottom she abandoned her inspection and wormed into the aperture as quickly as she could.

She brought a bulb of warm soup for Mota's lunch. When she entered Mota's vacuole, she noticed the stuffy, rank smell of age. She increased the ventilation. The rhythmic expansion and contraction of the air vessels made it sound like the room was breathing.

"Lunch, Mota!" she said in a cheerful tone.

Mota had taken all the clothes from one of the wall pockets, and was busy refolding everything and putting it back. She had done it at least ten times before, and with every repetition the clothes got a little more disordered. She looked up from her work and said anxiously, "Saji, where *were* you? I waited and waited. I thought something had happened to you!"

"I've only been gone an hour," Osaji said, her spirits falling. These reproaches were all she had gotten recently. She knew it would not stop unless she spent every hour of the day in the room. "Come eat your soup." She set it down on the little table they used to take their meals.

Mota looked in agitation at the clothing strewn all over the bed. She picked up a sweater she had just folded, shook it out, then put it down again. "Everything is all out of order," she said.

It was not the clothes that were out of order; it was something inside of Mota's mind. The behavior was simultaneously so unlike her grandmother and so very like her that Osaji felt trapped between laughter, dread, and impatience. Mota had always had a passion for tidiness; cleaning up after other people had been half her life, a way of expressing the love she couldn't put in words. Now it seemed like the trait was betraying her.

"I'll help you after lunch," Osaji said, but suspected that doing the task rather than completing it was what Mota needed.

A little reluctantly, the old woman came to the table and sat sipping her soup from the bulb. Her features looked stiff, her lips a little apart, stained with soup. Osaji tried to talk about the ark, but it was hard to keep it up alone. She kept fishing for responses and receiving none.

Suddenly Mota roused and got up restlessly. She started wandering around the room, looking for something in the wall pockets, underneath the bedclothes, in the washvac. After watching a while Osaji said, "What are you looking for?"

Mota paused as if having to search her mind for an answer. "My hand cream," she said at last.

"It's in the washvac, where it always is."

"Yes, of course." Mota went in the washvac, saw where it was, but did not pick it up. She came back out and settled in her chair.

The feeling in Osaji's stomach was much like the homesickness she felt for the Saltese Sea. It was a gnawing feeling that things were wrong, a yearning for a normality that was never coming back. And beneath it all lay buried anger at Mota for letting this confused stranger take over her body. An unworthy feeling.

"Would you like to go for a walk?" Osaji asked.

"No, thank you, sweetheart."

"Should I read to you?"

"If you want to," Mota said neutrally.

"I'm asking if *you* want me to." Osaji was unable to keep the desperate impatience from her voice. Mota fell silent. Feeling guilty, Osaji said, "Or would you like to take a nap?"

"Yes, that would be nice."

Mota had only agreed because it would be the least trouble. Nevertheless, Osaji seized upon it. She was feeling claustrophobic in this room, as if the smell was going to hang onto her forever. When she got up, Mota said anxiously, "Are you leaving?"

"Yes, I'm going to let you sleep." She came over and kissed the old woman's hair. Mota took her hand and said, "You're a good girl, Saji."

Controlling her inner rebellion, Osaji said, "Have a good rest, Mota."

When she was outside in the corridor, Osaji punched the wall with her fist, but it only yielded pliantly. "I am *not* a good girl," she said fiercely under her breath. How could Mota look at her—selfish and angry as she was—and say such a thing? It denied the reality of her resentment, and that diminished her. Her own grandmother, who ought to know her better than anyone in the world, saw not the individual Osaji but that generic thing, a "good girl." It made her feel like a mannikin, her personality negated.

¤

They drifted steadily westward, across a rocky plain that seemed to have no end. There was no navigation to do. The automated systems kept the ark at a steady depth and scanned for underwater obstacles, but there were none. Osaji made sure the machines were recording *Divernon*'s speed and direction; after that there was no need to visit the control pod more than once a day, to make sure nothing had changed. Nothing ever did.

An ark was supposed to work like a symphony, each person playing an indispensable part in the harmonic whole. But Jack made that impossible. He was unpredictable: one day torpid and morose, the next roaming the ark in a restless rage, throwing off sparks. All Osaji's attempts to suggest a useful role for him met a kind of egotistical nihilism.

"What's the point?" he said. "It only puts off the inevitable. We're going to die out here."

"We're going to die no matter where we are," Osaji said.

"Spare me the philosophy. Come on: how long before we run out of food and fuel?"

Puzzled by the question, she said, "Never."

"We can't restock out here."

"We don't need to, except for luxuries. The ark is self-sustaining."

"That's impossible. You would have invented a perpetual motion machine if that were so."

"The ark is not a machine," she protested. "It is not a closed system at all; it's an open one, based on autopoiesis. It's in a state of dynamic equilibrium with the sea. It exchanges chemicals in a chain, a process, that builds up complex molecules from simple ones."

"That's not possible. Not without fuel. The laws of thermodynamics are against it."

"Life violates thermodynamics all the time."

"Until it dies."

Back to that again. "All right, the ark will eventually die," Osaji admitted. "But not until after we do. Unless we don't maintain it. We are part of the system."

Even that failed to rouse any sense of responsibility in him. There was no alternative: Osaji had to try to do it all herself. And so her days became a numbing rush from one task to the next, never pausing to rest, always dragging her aching body on.

One day, she went to the clinic to get some sleeping medicine for Mota and found the drug supply ransacked. At first she stood staring at the pilfered wall pockets, unable to believe what she saw. Then her outrage boiled over.

She found Jack in the exercise vac, where he often spent time uselessly lifting weights. He was working the bench press with an aggressive intensity when she came in. She stood over him till he put the weights on their rack and sat up. "If it isn't the Guppy Girl," he said.

"It is impossible not to notice that the drugs are missing," she said.

"Oh yeah?"

She waited for him to look guilty, or excuse himself. He did neither. "Such egotism is…" she searched for a truly damning word, "antisocial. How can a man put his own temporary pleasure over the legitimate needs of others? What if one of us gets injured, or ill? You have robbed us of lifesaving cures that—"

"Oh, put a cork in it," Jack said.

Osaji's indignation exceeded her eloquence then. "You are an animal!" she cried. "You have stolen from my grandmother!"

Slowly, he stood up. He had no shirt on, and though he was short and wiry, his muscles were hard like knotted ropes. She took a step backward, for the first time realizing that he could easily overpower her. Fear urged her to flee, but anger made her stand her ground. "You see that tube there?" She pointed to the corridor outside. "On this side of it is yours, on the other side is mine. Don't cross it. If I catch you on my side, I swear I'll do you harm."

She turned and fled then. Stopping in the kitchen, she found a sharp knife. Feeling a little safer, she went to Mota's vac and found the old lady dozing peacefully. Osaji settled down, knife in hand, guarding the aperture.

Never had she faced such a situation. There were always personality conflicts in arks, but the social pressure kept them hidden. But here, for the first time in her life, Osaji was not part of a larger community. She was an independent being who needed to protect herself and her grandmother as best she could. Fingering the knife hilt, she hated Jack for making her into that most contemptible of all things, an egotist.

¤

She saw little of Jack in the time that followed. At first, she longed for him to overdose and drop dead, so she could push his body out into the sea and live the rest of her life in peace. But gradually she realized that he had at least been a kind of twisted distraction.

Her days came to revolve around Mota's constant needs for feeding, cleaning, and protection, and her other duties suffered. Immersed in age and infirmity day after day, Osaji herself began to feel dead and shriveled. She slept more than ever before, and woke with aching joints. When she hobbled to the mirror in the morning, she half expected to see white hair.

There was no one day when Mota took a turn for the worse, just a long series of imperceptible declines. It was not so much her hearing and sight failing as her will to hear or see. With her other senses went something Osaji could only describe as her sense of pleasure. No food tasted appealing to Mota, no sensation brought comfort, no activity brought content. Osaji could work until she was exhausted trying to satisfy her, all in vain. Mota's capacity for enjoyment was gone.

Osaji's only refuge was in the hydroponic nursery. Looking after the plants was a chore she actually liked. It took very little effort, but she lavished time on it anyway, because in the nursery she could pretend she wasn't on *Divernon*, or even on Ben.

One day she came as usual to tend the plants. The protective gear was still in the sac by the orifice, meaning no one was inside. She put on the hat, gloves, and dark glasses to shield her from the full-spectrum light, and entered.

Even with the goggles on, she squinted against the brilliance inside. The nursery was a sausage-shaped vesicle with long tubs of greenery lining each wall, and a tank down the middle. An adjoining sac held the deep, lightless pool where underwater species grew in a chemical broth that mimicked their natural sea-vent habitat.

She started down the row of greenery, pinching off dead leaves and spraying the plants with nutrient-water. As she parted one thicket of foliage, she noticed something peculiar. On the counter behind the screen of plants stood a row of glass jars full of cloudy liquid. They had not been there when she last tended the plants, she was sure. As she reached out to pick one up, a voice behind her grated, "Don't touch that."

Jolted, she whirled around. Jack was sitting on the floor behind her, hidden by a tank.

He raised his hands and said, "Lower your weapon. I surrender."

She realized she was holding the plant sprayer in front of her like a gun, as if to spritz him with water. Ridiculous as it was, she didn't lower it. "What do you want?" she demanded.

Stiffly, he got up. "I want a joint and a ticket out of here, for all the good it does me."

He wasn't wearing any protective gear. She said, "A man should be wearing glasses."

With a harried look he said, "Don't you ever let up?"

"But the radiation is dangerous in here!"

"Don't worry, this is the only room that doesn't seem dim as a dungeon to me."

He took a step forward. She pointed the sprayer at him, and he stopped. "Okay, okay," he said. "Look, we can't go on like this. We're the only two damned people in this ship. We've got to call a cease fire."

Suspicious of this new ploy, she said, "So someone can go on raiding our drugs?"

"I apologize for that." He didn't look apologetic, more like desperately irritated at himself. "The thing is—I'm going bugfuddled crazy. I haven't been clean and sober at the same time in about ten years. It doesn't improve me. That's why—" He nodded at the jars behind her plants.

"What are they?" she said.

"I'm making wine."

Osaji said, "You shouldn't keep them here."

Bitterly sarcastic, he said, "Sorry for polluting your sanctum."

"No, I mean, they won't ferment properly in the light. They should be somewhere dark and cool."

He paused. "I knew that." He came over and gathered the jars off the counter. It seemed like he was about to leave, but he stopped. Then, eyes fixed on something beyond her, he began to talk in a rush, as if he were bleeding words.

"During the war, I was on a ship called *Viper*. It was a godless piece of junk, really. We used to joke about it, called it the *Vindow Viper*. One day they sent us in to take over a communication station owned by an asteroid-mining company. Only it turned out to be a secret military installation. They blew our piece-of-shit cruiser to bits before we had time to wet our pants. Eleven of us managed to escape in space suits, with only a marker buoy to hang to. We waited there for rescue. You know what it's like in space? It's dark, and your body has no weight. There's nothing to smell, or see, or feel. If you kick, nothing happens. It's just yourself all alone, thinking till your brain echoes like the whole universe.

"We had a big argument while we were waiting for rescue. Some of them thought the oxygen would last longer if we linked our tanks together. I was against it, me and two others. The rest decided to do it, and eventually persuaded everyone but me. It was four days before a ship picked us up. Their oxygen ran out at three and a half. If I'd helped them, I would have died too. I used to think I was the smart one, the lucky one."

Osaji was so taken aback she forgot to point the sprayer at him.

"Look," he said, "I came to this godforsaken planet to shed my self like an old dirty T-shirt into the laundry. I was hunting for a clean break. I wanted to be a new person, but the old person sticks to me like a bad smell. My past is something I stepped in long ago and can't get off my shoe."

This only made Osaji's own self-pity well up to match his. "You are not the only one trapped here unwillingly. Do you think I do all this work for pleasure? Do you think I want to maintain this ark and wash and dress and feed someone as if I were some kind of appliance? No one would choose this. It is degrading."

Finally he seemed to focus on her. "Then for God's sake, give me something to do! If I have to sit around thinking any more, I'm going to start chewing my leg off."

Suspicious at this change, she said, "What can a spacer do?"

"I don't know. Teach me, while I still have a few brain cells left alive."

It came to her then: the job she most wanted rid of. "I can teach the spacer to go outside."

To her surprise, he blanched. "No, you don't want me out there. I'd just be a drag on you."

"Our breathers are easier to use than yours. You don't have to carry oxygen; the breather extracts it from the water. And it's not like space. When you kick, something happens."

"Listen," he said, "I've got to tell you something. Truth is, I was a complete screwup as a spacer. You see, I couldn't turn off my mind. I couldn't stop thinking of consequences, and caring about them. I couldn't stop seeing the danger, and the stupidity, and the venality, and the faces...."

He had wandered off again, into some haunted territory of his mind. To pull him back, she said, "There are no faces in the sea. No venality either."

With a hoarse laugh he said, "Well, that leaves danger and stupidity."

"Only if you bring them."

"Shit! Shit! Shit!" he said.

5. Through Shadow Valley

The aperture to the outside was located in the floor at the very bottom of the globe. The trick to getting through it was, once suited up, to take a little leap and plunge in feet first, as if jumping into a pool. Osaji had never thought of it as a skill till she watched Jack trying to follow her out. He got stuck halfway, struggling ineptly and letting air escape in big bubbles that rolled up the ark's side. Trying not to laugh, Osaji grasped one flailing ankle and gave a sharp tug, ignoring the curses emanating from her radio earpiece.

He was awkward and jerky in the water, and she had to make him swim to and fro a while to get the hang of the flippers. Then she took him on a tour of the ark's exterior, showing him the emergency entry pores and the scars of their encounter with the heat plumes and the mountain.

With Jack beside her, the darkness no longer seemed so oppressive. It gave her the courage to do something she had not contemplated in a long time: gather water samples. They had to be taken at some distance, to avoid contamination from the cloud of organic molecules the ark gave off.

As soon as they left the sheltering bulge of the ark, they were enveloped in a dark so inky that all direction disappeared. Osaji stripped the covers from the phosphor patches on her suit so Jack could see where she was. She turned back to show him how to do the same, but he had already figured it out.

Though they swam slowly, the ark soon dwindled to a dim ball behind. It was icy cold. Jack switched on the searchlamp, but the beam just disappeared into water in every direction. They seemed suspended in nothingness.

Jack muttered, "A dark illimitable ocean without bound, where length, breadth, time and place are lost."

"What does that mean?" Osaji asked.

"It's poetry, kid. Damn spooky, that's what it means."

Osaji took the sampling bottle from the pack at her belt and held it out at arm's length as she swam, releasing the cap. As she was covering it again, something touched her face.

She gave a startled exclamation, and was suddenly blinded by the light as Jack turned it on her. "What is it?" he said.

"Turn that off!"

He did, but light still danced before her dazzled eyes. For a terrifying moment, she couldn't even tell up from down. She blinked until the dim glow of Jack's phosphor patches swam into view. "Can you see the ark?" she said.

"Right there," he said, presumably pointing with an invisible arm.

She saw it then as well, dimly, farther off than it should be. But as she started for it, Jack said, "Hey, where are you going?"

The photism she had been following vanished, and as she turned, the real *Divernon* swam into view. If he had not been there to stop her, she might have wandered off, chasing a mirage.

"Let's go back," she said, rattled.

They raced back as fast as they could swim. When they were inside again, he said, "What the hell happened out there?"

"This swimmer thought she felt a heat tendril."

"What's that?"

"A current of warmer water. No one else felt it?"

"Warm! You've got to be kidding."

"It must have been an illusion, then."

Still, she went to check the ark's temperature records. They were disappointingly flat. She had to tamp down the tiny updraft of hope that it had been a hint of geothermal activity. Another rift zone would mean a site for colonization—an energy source for life.

She couldn't entirely suppress the thought. The currents here were robust. They had to be driven by something. Just the possibility was like an infusion of energy. She felt buoyant and excited as she went to check on Mota, like the little girl she had once been, running to tell her grandmother of some discovery.

Mota roused from an open-eyed doze and smiled sweetly when Osaji told her what had just happened. "That's nice, dear," she said. Stiffly, she rose from her chair, and Osaji saw that the back of her dress was soaked.

"Mota, you've wet yourself," she said, shocked.

"No, I haven't," Mota said, turning so Osaji couldn't see it.

"Here, I'll help you change." Osaji tried to make her voice neutral.

"No, no," Mota said, "don't worry. I can do it myself." She stood looking around uncertainly, as if she had never seen the room before. Silently, Osaji went to the wall pocket and found some dry clothes. She felt irrationally humiliated by this new infirmity. It was so unlike Mota.

Mota took a long time changing clothes in the washvac. Osaji sat at the table, all at once too enervated to move. Her bubble of high spirits was leaking air, and she was sinking into stagnant water again.

The trip outside revived Jack's fund of hare-brained schemes. "What if we were to rig a really big antenna?" he said. "Maybe we could generate a low-frequency signal that could penetrate all this water and ice."

Osaji was skeptical that any length of antenna would help them, but it did no harm to try. So she helped him string floats on a braided carbon-steel mooring line and paid it out into the water. Before long *Divernon* was trailing a long tail of wire.

It did not improve their communications. The radio still hissed white noise. But the antenna did succeed in an unexpected way.

As the current carried them inexorably westward, the seafloor landscape became more rugged. The sonar showed the hunched shoulders of hills below them, concealed by inky water. Then one day the bottom dropped out of the world.

On a routine check of the control pod, Osaji was startled to see no sonar reading at all. Going back to check the record, she found that the soundings had stopped only two hours before. When a diagnostic turned up no problem with the equipment, she came to the only plausible conclusion: they had been swept over the edge of an underwater chasm. The ark was caught in a gentle eddy, and as it floated backward her conjecture was confirmed, for the sonar picked up the edge of fluted organ-pipe cliffs dropping away into darkness so deep the signal could not reach the bottom.

By then, she and Jack were both watching the screen, mesmerized. "What should we do?" Osaji asked. It was the first navigation decision they had had to make.

"What are the options?" Jack said.

"We could go down, or stay at our present depth. If we stay, we'll probably pick up the westward current again. If we drop down...."

"Yes?" he prompted when she failed to continue.

"Well, there is no telling. There might be no current down there. Then we would just come up again. There might be a current that would sweep us some place we don't want to be."

"As opposed to now?" Jack said ironically.

"That is a point."

Often, decisions like this took hours, because everyone was afraid to be first to voice an opinion, and they talked until a consensus emerged without anyone having to say it aloud. But Jack suffered no inhibitions about expressing himself. "I say go for it. Take the plunge," he said. "What good are we doing out here if we don't take time to see the sights?"

She smiled at him, because she agreed.

He stared at her open-mouthed till she said, "Is something wrong?"

"I don't think I've ever seen you smile before," he said.

That made her feel self-conscious, so she turned to the controls and input the sequence of commands that would take them downward.

As soon as they dropped below the edge of the cliff, they lost their current. They were close enough to the cliff that the side-sounding sonar could show an image of the stately columns of basalt plunging into unknowable depths below. Osaji pushed back her chair and rose.

"Where are you going?" Jack said.

"It will take a long time to sink," she said. "We have to adjust to the pressure as we go down. It could be hours."

He couldn't tear himself from the screens, so she left him there, watching.

In the end, it took three days. As they descended, the water temperature slowly rose one degree, and Osaji's hopes rose with it. When the sonar finally picked up the bottom, they both sat watching the screen intently while the detail improved scan by scan. What it showed was only another tumbled slope of boulders leading down to a rumpled seafloor. "Look at the edges of the rocks," Osaji said, pointing at the screen. "They are sharp, not eroded. That means this area could be geologically active."

But they saw nothing else in any way remarkable.

They did pick up a new current, sweeping them slowly north along the line of the cliffs. The next day, the side sonar picked up another trace opposite them—the other side of the canyon, closing in fast. As the gorge became narrower, the current sped up, and Osaji began to fear that the gap would become too narrow for them to pass.

"What should we do?" she said.

"Ride it out, I guess," Jack said, his eyes glued to the monitors. "Like whitewater ballooning. Yee-ha."

Soon the giant cliffs were marching by, close on either side. For a moment the sonars showed nothing but rock in every direction—they were being swept around a curve. A gap appeared ahead. They were heading toward it.

Then all motion seemed to stop. The cliffs were behind them. They had entered onto the floor of a dark, hidden valley.

¤

At first it seemed that they had just exchanged one lightless wasteland for another. Day by day they traveled northwest, their rocky surroundings unchanged. But there was a difference: as if they had passed a wall severing them forever from home.

Even Mota seemed to be drifting into another world Osaji could not enter, or imagine. As her memory failed, the old woman lost her ability to detect a sequence of events, to tell the *before* from the *after*; and with sequence gone, time itself disappeared. At first her own confusion frightened her, and she asked constantly what time it was, as if to force her experiences into order. But as she grew accustomed to it, she learned to exist in a bath of time where all the past was present simultaneously. She began to confuse Osaji with long-dead people from her childhood. Whenever it happened, Osaji corrected her more sharply than she should have; but she couldn't help it. The reaction came from deep down, like the reflex to breathe, or defend her life—except it was her individuality she was defending. As Mota's failing senses saw her less and less distinctly, Osaji felt like she was disappearing, turning invisible as water.

She was in Mota's vac when a shudder and a jerk went through the ark. "Did you feel that?" she said.

"What, dear?"

Osaji was very attuned to *Divernon*'s motions by now, and knew something was amiss. There was a faint rushing sound that seemed to come from everywhere at once. She sprinted up to the control pod, arriving only moments before Jack did. "*You* felt it," she said, forgetting to be polite.

"Damn straight I did."

Osaji's biggest fear, that they had collided with something, turned out not to be true. *Divernon* had come to a sudden halt in mid-stream. The sound she heard was water flowing past the membrane.

"The antenna!" Jack said.

Osaji had forgotten all about it. She saw now what he meant: one or more of the floats must have come loose and allowed the line to sink. They had been dragging a line along the seafloor, and now it was caught on something.

"We should have brought it in long ago," Osaji said, reproaching herself for irresponsibility. "Now we will lose a good mooring cable. We will have to cut it away."

"Well, maybe we can salvage part of it," Jack said.

"Do you think someone would be willing to go out there to cut it?"

"Not by myself," Jack said. "I'd go with you."

They planned it out carefully this time, since there would be more risk than their last job had entailed. The combination of tether and current had brought *Divernon* down closer to the bottom than it ought to be, and as soon as it was freed it would float up. They needed to be sure not to lose it.

The water was noticeably warmer to Osaji. It was, of course, just as black. Lit by their headlamps, the mooring cable stretched taut, a straight line leading diagonally downward, punctuated by floats every few yards. They set out, swimming along it. The farther they went before cutting it, the more of it they would be able to salvage.

The ark disappeared into the darkness behind them. Osaji noticed that she could now see the narrow beam of light from her headlamp; there was something dissolved in the water. For some reason, she did not want to get close to the bottom. The thought of monstrous rock shapes below her, hidden since the beginning of eternity, filled her with dread. She was about to suggest that they had come far enough and should cut the cable when Jack said, "What's that?"

"What?" she said, drawing in her feet out of fear that they would touch something.

"Turn on the searchlight," he said.

When she did, she gasped.

They were surrounded by glass towers. Not solid glass, but intricate meshworks of spun filaments that glinted silver and azure in the beam of Osaji's light. As the searchlight touched the nearest ones, they seemed to ignite in a cascade, as if conducting the light from one glass strand to the next, till the entire landscape around them glowed. Latticework turrets towered over them; gazebos and arcades of glistering mesh lay below. In the distance, some were broken and toppled, but the ones nearby looked perfectly preserved. It was like a city of hoarfrost, magnified to the size of monuments.

As her light played over the intricate structures, Osaji could not help the impression that it was a sort of architecture, created by design. But what strange intelligence would have built a monument down here, in a lightless gulf where no one would ever see it?

Even Jack at her side, after an initial exhalation of astonishment, was awed into silence. He slowly swam forward, and Osaji followed, drawn to touch, to be *in* the tracery sculpture, to see it from every angle.

They glided through arches that dwarfed them, down a tube woven of glowing geometric webs, and looked up from inside an open spiral that towered into the black water sky. They swam along lacework corridors, into honeycomb spheres of overlapping glass threads. Nowhere was there any sign of life. Not a thing moved but themselves.

In a glowing, cathedral-like space they found three hexagonal glass pillars, of uneven heights, whose surfaces were inscribed with patterns like worm tracks. Jack swam around the cluster of stelae, then said what Osaji was thinking: "Do you suppose it's writing?"

"I don't know. We ought to record it."

All thought of cutting the mooring line was gone now. It had been a stroke of the most astonishing luck that it had caught just here. They swam back toward it, chilled and eager to fetch some recording devices.

When they emerged into the womb of the ark and stripped off their diving gear, the awe that had held them in silence broke, and Jack let out a whoop of exhilaration. "Holy crap, that was the most amazing thing I've ever seen. Who do you think they were?"

He was leaping to the assumption that Osaji had tried cautiously to suppress. "It did not look natural," she admitted. "But it might have been a coral or something similar."

"Great big humping underwater spiders," Jack speculated. "But spiders that could read and write. Where's the camera?"

Osaji was rubbing her feet, which were the color and temperature of oysters. "We ought to warm up before going back. If one of us could heat some soup, the other will find the camera."

They were about to split up when the ark gave a shudder and moved. The cable was slipping. "No!" Jack shouted at it. "Don't give way!"

It was too late. There was a jerk, then suddenly the ark was rising, floating free again.

Jack let out a stream of profanity more heartfelt than any Osaji had heard from him. "Can't we drop an anchor?" he said. Osaji leaped to draw in the line, but long before they managed to attach an anchor to it, they both knew their chance was gone. The ark had floated on, and they were left with nothing but their memory of what they had seen.

¤

That evening Osaji came down from the control pod, where she had been studying the sonar readings to see if they had recorded evidence of the glass city, to find Jack and Mota together in the kitchen.

"Mota!" she exclaimed. "What are you doing here?"

"Hello, dear," Mota said brightly. "Do you remember Yamada?"

Osaji felt embarrassed that Jack had seen Mota so confused, and was about to usher her back to her vac when he stopped her. "We've been having an interesting conversation. How come you've been hiding away this charming lady?"

Mota giggled like a girl.

Osaji stared at Jack, suspicious that he was mocking both Mota and her.

"She's been telling me about one round when a man named Sabo transferred from her ark to another one," Jack said, then turned to Mota. "So what happened next?"

She looked confused. "Oh, nothing in particular."

It was like most of Mota's stories these days; they trailed off into pointlessness. Osaji stirred restlessly, wanting to get Mota away.

"I see," Jack said. "Well, more power to Sabo. I say that's how a man ought to act."

Mota beamed at him fondly. He leaned over and whispered to Osaji, "Who the hell is Yamada?"

"Her brother. My great-uncle," Osaji said.

"Bit of a scapegrace, I take it?"

Osaji nodded. "He was her favorite sibling."

"I'm honored to be him," he said, and rose to fetch a bottle from a cupboard. "In view of the occasion, I think we ought to have some wine."

"It's too soon," Osaji warned him. "It will taste awful."

"Then it should suit me nicely," he said, and broke the seal. She watched him pour some into a glass. He smelled it and winced, then took a mouthful and downed it. He grimaced, then glared at the glass resentfully.

"It is vile, true?" Osaji said.

"On the contrary," he said. "It's a belligerent little vintage with a sarcastic attitude. I like it very much." He took another swig.

Osaji took down a glass and held it out. Jack poured her a glassful, and she took a sip. It was vinegary and revolting.

"Care for some?" Jack asked Mota.

"Oh, don't give it to her," Osaji said.

"She wants some. An adventurous spirit, I see," he said, and poured her a tiny amount. She sipped, and made a sour face. Jack laughed. "You're never going to trust me again now, are you?"

"You're always playing jokes on me," Mota said with mock severity.

"Come on, Mota, this man is a bad influence," Osaji said, rising.

"Bring her back soon. I'll turn her into a lush yet."

"Not with that wine," Osaji said.

When she had gotten Mota safely back to her vac, Osaji returned to the kitchen. Jack was studying the sonar printouts she had brought down from the control pod. They showed next to nothing. The glass structures had been too fragile and airy to give a clear return.

"I'd think I had imagined the whole thing, if you hadn't seen it too," Jack said.

"Even if we ever get back, no one will believe us."

They continued drinking the wine in silence.

Osaji felt as if a vast weight of sadness were hanging above her, pressing inward, making it hard to breathe. "Jack," she said, "we ought to make an effort to remember. Think of those people, or whatever they were, who built the city. They created all that, and now they are forgotten, so forgotten it's as if they never existed. And now we don't even have any proof we saw the city they made. We owe it to them to remember, to make them real. It's the least we can do."

He gave a slight, bitter smile. "As if we mattered ourselves."

She saw what he meant. They were next to forgotten as well. The farther they traveled from home, the less they would be remembered. No doubt they were already given up for lost; soon they would drift farther and farther into the night, until all trace of their existence disappeared. Nothing would remain in the end.

"If everyone has forgotten us, do you suppose we'll still exist?" Osaji said.

He stirred restlessly. "You don't have enough to forget. Try living a life like mine. You'll know then, memory's a disease."

He was silent a while, and she thought he was going to say no more, but he went on, "If those city builders thought they'd be remembered, they were crazy. Forgetting is what nature does best. The universe is a huge forgetting machine. It erases information no matter how hard we try to hang onto it. How could it be any different? What if the memory of everything that ever happened still existed? The universe would be clogged with information, so packed with it we couldn't move. We'd be paralyzed, because every moment we ever lived would still be with us. It would be hell."

Osaji thought of Mota, in whom memory was the most evanescent thing of all. Already Osaji existed only fleetingly for Mota, and Jack was not even a separate person, only the shadow of the long-dead Yamada. And soon Mota, then all of them, would arrive at the ultimate forgetting toward which they were traveling. They were all swimming temporarily in a sea of darkness, and then they would be gone.

The sadness pressed in, crushing her. Her eyes were tightly closed, but seawater was leaking from them anyway. It was for the lost city, for poor *Divernon*, for Mota, and for herself, the most futile of them all.

Jack reached across the table and took her hand. "Don't listen to me, kid. I don't think I'm going to forget you. Not a chance."

She clutched his hand as if he were the only thing that made her real.

6. Garden of the Deep

It was impossible for Osaji to keep Mota and Jack apart in the weeks that followed. Whenever Osaji's back was turned, Mota would creep out looking for him, and when she found him he teased her, told her inappropriate jokes, and fed her the sweet treats that were the only food she really craved. She would sit in the kitchen playing hostess to him, so polite that only Osaji could tell it was play-acting, like a little girl pretending to be an adult. Gradually, Osaji learned to stop resenting it.

As they traveled, she reduced the ark's cruising depth and pored over the sensor readings in hopes of finding another underwater city. Though they now kept an anchor ready to drop on a moment's notice, she saw no hint of anything but barren rock and rumpled lava on the seafloor.

Then one day the water temperature shot up. When she discovered it, Osaji consulted the sonar, but the images were fuzzy and hard to interpret. She went to find Jack. "I think a man should check to see what's outside," she said.

"Why a man?" he said, to be irritating.

"Because someone else needs to be inside ready to throw the anchor out."

They both went down to the hatch pod. Only seconds after he disappeared through the aperture, her radio earpiece started emitting ear-blistering vulgarities.

"What is it?" she asked.

There was no answer for several seconds. Then, "There's *light* out here."

The thought that there might be erupting lava made her hopeful. Then the more likely explanation occurred to her. "You mean the ark?"

"Well, yes, it's glowing like gangbusters. But I meant the trees."

"*Trees?*"

"There's a prigging forest out here!"

"Should one drop the anchor?"

"Yes! Then get your ass out here. No offense."

When she emerged from the ark, the sight struck her dumb. The ark hovered over an undulating landscape of dimly glowing lifeforms that covered the seafloor thickly in every direction, till they disappeared on the dark horizon. When she trained the searchlamp on them, the greenish phosphor glow disappeared and the biotic canopy proved to be made up of pinkish fronds gently undulating in the current, attached to tall stalks that looked in every way like tree trunks, except that they were larger than any tree she had seen.

Osaji and Jack swam down till they were hovering over the fronds, and could see their scale. The central rib of each branch was twenty to thirty feet long, and the splayed-out fern covered an area as wide as *Divernon*'s diameter. Jack reached out to touch the nearest one, and with a violent jerk the whole thing retracted into its tube, leaving behind a cloud of disturbed water. Several adjacent brushtops retracted as well.

"They are tubeworms!" Osaji said in astonishment. But tubeworms of a size she had never dreamed of.

"What do they eat?" Jack said, still rattled by the violent reaction he had stimulated.

"Not us. They are filter feeders. But it would be easy to get pulled down into the tube and crushed."

"You're telling me."

They swam down into the space thus cleared. Below the palmlike tops, the tubes were ribbed and hard, and so wide around that Osaji and Jack could not span them with their arms, even by linking hands. The trunks were crusted with orange and yellow growths that looked for all the world like fungus—except when touched, they moved.

Osaji felt something brush her face, but could see nothing. "Turn off your light a moment," she said. When Jack complied, they found themselves in a wholly different world. The water under the tubeworm canopy was alive with glowing filaments that outlined segmented bodies, hourglass-shaped bags, lacy things like floating doilies, others like paintbrushes or fringed croissants. It was as if the trees were strung with optic fiber ornaments, or fireflies in formation. When Osaji switched her light on again, they all disappeared. "Jellies!" she said. "The light goes right through them."

Lower down, there was a dense undergrowth that showed a riot of colors in their lights. There were frilly orchidlike things, huge bushes of feathers, clusters of translucent orange bottles, in one place a fan lazily waving to and fro, stirring the still water. "Look, your spiders!" Osaji called out, training her light on a china-white creature with six spindly legs, picking its way over a thing that looked like a brain.

When they turned around at last, Jack swam ahead, with Osaji lighting the way. She barely saw the thing that came arrowing out of the darkness at him. It hit him in the chest and drove him backward through the water so fast that Osaji lost him for a moment. With panic pounding in her ears, she swept her light around and saw him, seemingly impaled on a tubeworm trunk with a thrashing, snakelike body attached to his chest. She churned through the water toward him, and with no weapon but her light, she gave the creature a blow. It did not let go or cease whipping its paddle-shaped tail. Jack now had ahold of it and was trying to pull it away, a maneuver that would almost surely tear his suit. She grasped the paddletail near the front and squeezed with all her strength. It took what seemed like minutes, but the creature finally went limp and let go. She shone her light on it. It had no head, just a giant sucker where a mouth should be. With an exclamation of revulsion, she threw it away and it floated downward into the blackness.

"Is your suit all right?" she said, inspecting the place where the paddletail had attached. To make sure, she took some repair goo from her utility belt and smeared it on.

"Never mind the suit. What about *me*?" Jack said irritably.

"Are you all right?"

"Some wear and tear, thanks for asking."

"Let's get back."

They could see the ark through the branches above, like a bright full moon. Its bioluminescent bacteria were thriving in this nutrient-rich water. When they were inside, she inspected the bruise on Jack's chest but determined that no ribs were broken. "We need to be more careful," she said.

"You have a way with understatement," he answered.

They spent three days documenting the new world they had discovered before floating cn. At first they stayed outside a great deal as they floated, anxious not to miss anything; then Jack figured out how to rig a camera on the outside of the ark so they could watch from the comfort of the control pod. Osaji marveled that she had never thought of such a thing—but then, in the Saltese Sea there was nothing to see outside and no light to see it by anyway. Everything there was focused inward.

The underwater woodland of tube worms slowly gave way to a wide plain of sea grass. They sat atop the ark and watched the glowing prairie undulate in the currents, while their light beams picked out raylike creatures circling in the updrafts above. One day there was a shower of mineral particles. Pebble-sized bits pattered around them like raindrops, and soon a mist of smaller ash descended. It was what was fertilizing this oasis of life.

Eventually the land began to rise and they saw the first of the smoker chimneys belching out thick clouds of steam and dissolved minerals from deep within the planet's crust. Here, a spiny red growth dominated the ecosystem, like a branched bottle brush the size of a tower. In the sediment below the spine trees grew blooming fields of small tubeworms like chrysanthemums and daisies, and enigmatic things shaped like mesh stockings. They saw many more of the whiplike paddletails, always swimming upstream in the direction opposite to the one the ark was floating. Occasionally, some of the brainless things would attach to the downstream side of the ark, their tails still paddling frantically as if to push the ark against the current. Then Osaji and Jack would have to go outside and weed the ark.

What they never saw, though they looked all the time, was any evidence of the species that had built the glass city.

"I don't get this," Jack said. "We find a city with no life, and life with no city."

Osaji wanted to be outside all the time now. The ark's interior seemed drab and claustrophobic, and she rushed through her duties there to get into the water again.

They were moored on the edge of a mazy badlands of extinct smokers, their sides streaked like candles with brightly colored deposits of copper, sulphur, and iron, when the accident happened. Osaji was preparing to go outside when she bustled into Mota's vac and found the old lady lying on the floor, conscious but unable to speak. Panicky, Osaji knelt beside her. "Mota, what happened?"

Mota only looked up with round, watery eyes. Her mouth worked; nothing came out but a thin line of saliva. It filled Osaji with horror to see her grandmother so robbed of humanity. She jumped up and raced out to find Jack.

When they tried to move Mota to the bed, she groaned in pain, her eyes wild and staring. "She's probably broken something," Jack said.

"What can we do?" Osaji said.

"Not a lot," Jack said grimly. "Make her comfortable. Wait here, I'll be right back."

He disappeared. Osaji sat on the floor holding Mota's hand. Mota gripped back, hanging on as if a strong current were sweeping her from the world. "We'll try to do something for you, Mota," Osaji said. "Just relax, don't worry."

Jack came back with a little sack of pills. "Here, see if she can swallow this," he said.

"What is it?" Osaji frowned at the pill he handed her.

"Codeine," he said.

So he hadn't consumed all of them. She glanced at him, but he had turned away.

She managed to get Mota to swallow the pill and wash it down from a cup with a straw. Almost at once, far quicker than the drug could have taken effect, Mota closed her eyes and relaxed. They waited till they were sure she was asleep, then moved her onto the bed.

When they had done all they could, Jack said, "You want me to leave or stay?"

At first Osaji was unsure of what she wanted. Then at last she said, "Stay."

So began a long ordeal of waiting. From time to time Mota would rouse and reach out for one of them; it didn't seem to matter which one. As Osaji sat looking at Mota's face, she was forced to think: I longed to be free of her, yet now I don't want her to die.

More than anyone Osaji knew, Mota had forsaken her own wants in order to live for others. Selflessness. It was a virtue; everyone said so. And yet, it was as if her individuality had slowly withered away from neglect over the years. She had spent a lifetime making herself transparent, till she had no substance of her own, and all you saw was the substance of others seen through her.

As Osaji studied Mota's face, it seemed impossible that those mild and vacant features had ever known obsession, rage, or remorse. Had Mota ever believed deeply in something, or taken risks? She had never spoken of herself—never even known herself, perhaps. Now she never would.

"She doesn't deserve this," Osaji said softly.

After a few seconds, Jack said, "No one does. But we all get it, in the end."

"I mean, to die out here, so far from everyone else. She lived for other people. Without them, there's nothing left of her."

There was a long silence. At last Jack said, "Just to warn you, this takes a long time. It's messy and hard. People fight it. Even her."

He was right. She struggled painfully against the ebbing of her life. Osaji and Jack took turns sitting with her and giving her medicine when she roused. They were soon worn out, but still she hung on. At the very end she looked up at Osaji, and seemed to recognize her. "Why is it so dark?" she said.

"Don't worry about it, Mota. We're right here with you."

Her hand contracted around Osaji's, and she said, "I wish...."

Osaji never found out what she wished.

Osaji dressed Mota's body in her favorite clothes and they wrapped her in one of the weighted nets used for burial in the Saltese Sea. At home, they would have laid her among barren rocks to nourish the microorganisms, so she could become mother to all the life that followed. Here, they laid her in a spot that was already like a garden: a cushiony bed of tubeworm flowers. Then they raised the anchor and floated on.

It was the next day before the grief came. Osaji had gone to Mota's vac to clean up, and found in one of the wall pockets a sweater that Mota had worn till it was the shape of her. When Osaji held it up, it seemed so empty, and yet still full of her. She hugged it tight, and it gave off the smell of love.

All at once, Osaji missed Mota so intensely her throat squeezed tight around her breath, and around her heart, and tears pried their way out between her eyelids. She knew then she had lost the only person who would ever love her just for being herself. It was the only *inadvertent* love she would ever know—love as deep as the genes that knit them together. There would never be anyone else who simply *had* to love her.

They had come to a place where, far away through the water, they could see the flickering light of eruptions from a line of undersea volcanoes. They went outside to sit on top of the ark and watch.

"Do you believe in an afterlife?" Osaji said.

Jack paused, as if considering whether to lie. At last he said, "No."

"So when we die, that's the end?"

"We can only hope." After a few seconds he added, "Sorry. I ought to give you comforting platitudes, I suppose."

"No. I hope death is the end, too. Because if Mota knew we'd left her so far from everything familiar, she'd feel lost and scared forever."

A paddletail shot past them, swimming upstream. "Where do you suppose they're going?" Osaji said.

"Nowhere. They're just crazy. Always swimming against the current, as if—" Suddenly, he stopped.

"What?" she said.

"I've got an idea."

It was as crazy as all his other ideas. But at least it didn't require technology they didn't have, or skills they couldn't acquire. It wasn't a spacer idea, it was a Bennish idea.

They set about gathering paddletails. They used sheets of plastic scavenged from inside the ark—vat covers, tarpaulins, anything that could be spared. They spread them wide to catch the creatures speeding past. Once affixed to a surface, the paddletails held on tenaciously, still whipping their tails against the current. As their numbers increased, Osaji and Jack repositioned some to the upstream side of the ark, where they strained against the lines holding them as if they were in harness. Others went to the downstream side to push against the ark like so many flailing motors.

The moment when *Divernon* started moving slowly against the current, Osaji and Jack slapped each other's hands in triumph, then swam to catch up with the ark.

For many days they experimented and refined the rigging before they were satisfied with the way their herd of snakes was deployed. It looked absurd, as if their washing were spread out in a tattered array all around the ark. But it pulled them slowly, inexorably, backward the way they had come.

They still couldn't steer, of course. The paddletails would go only one direction, upstream. But if they kept going long enough, they would take *Divernon* home.

Back they went, over the seagrass plains, past the tubeworm jungle. Every day Osaji went to the control pod to search for the best current—strong enough to keep the paddletails going, weak enough not to overpower them. Every day she and Jack went outside to catch more, fearful their present herd would die. In a few weeks they began to discover eggs embedded in the rough outer membrane of the ark, the spawn of their captives. Uncertain of the paddletail life cycle, they gathered some to raise in one of their tanks and left the rest to hatch outside, in hopes that the creatures' instincts would bring them back to spawn in the place where they were born.

They must have passed the glass city, but they did not see it and could not stop to search. They rose up over the edge of the rift valley and into the primeval waste with some misgiving. The current was much gentler here, so they made better headway; but the paddletails did not thrive. Carefully they nursed along their second generation, experimenting to see what they ate. One day, having tried everything else, Jack poured some of his home-brewed rotgut into their tank, and they went into a frenzy trying to drink it.

"Kindred souls!" he whooped. "They need to be plastered to stay alive!"

After that, Osaji and Jack devoted as much biomass as they could spare to the production of alcohol. Across the dark plain, *Divernon* became like a floating distillery. "At least *something* around here is lit," Jack observed.

Despite their best efforts, their creatures were much depleted by the time the sonar began to show the outline of mountains ahead. Remembering the strength of the current that had swept them through the gap, Osaji worried that their paddletail propulsion system wouldn't have the power to get them through. She and Jack were both in the control pod when they made the first attempt. The paddletails pulled them unerringly toward the pass where the current flowed strongest; but as the water velocity increased, the ark slowed. Barely a hundred yards from the gap, they came to a complete stop. The paddletails, pushing as hard as they could, could not draw them through.

"We've got to drop down out of the current," Osaji said. "They can't do it. We're going to wear them out."

"Wait," Jack said, looking at the screen. "What's that above us?"

"The ice," Osaji said, dread in her heart. Here, at the mountain pass, it was perilously close.

"Go up," he said.

She shook her head. "We could get trapped." People had warned of it all her life.

"It's our only choice," he said.

So, quelling her fear, she input the command that would dump ballast water from the tank and send them slowly upward.

As they rose, she watched the image of the ice's underside grow clearer on the screen. It was not smooth, but carved into channels, with knifelike ridges projecting down like the keels of enormous, frozen boats. The water temperature was falling. The cold made the paddletails sluggish; soon they would cease to pull. "This isn't going to work," Osaji said softly.

"Hang on," Jack said.

They were almost close enough to touch the ice when they felt the stirring of a countercurrent flowing east. The paddletails, paralyzed with cold, did not respond. *Divernon* started floating toward the mountains again, this time swept on the breath of the sea.

Ahead, the sonar showed that the ice and the mountain peaks converged. "Get into one of those channels in the ice," Jack suggested.

"But what if—"

"Just try it, for chrissake! What have we got to lose?"

They entered a deep cleft with ice walls on either side. As the mountains rose to block their way, a floor formed beneath them, cutting them off from below. Now, there was no longer an option of dropping back down. They were in a tunnel of ice and rock. Ahead, the walls closed in. They felt a gentle jostle, then heard the sound of water rushing past the membrane.

Divernon had come to a stop in the stream. The passage was too narrow, and they were stuck.

They sat motionless for a few moments. Then Jack said, "Sorry."

"No!" Osaji said. "We can't give up now. I'm going to vent air. Maybe it will push us past this narrow spot."

The first jet of air had no effect. "Keep going," Jack said. "Less air, smaller balloon. Maybe it'll shrink us down to size."

They had vented an alarming amount when *Divernon* stirred, slipped, and then floated on down the tunnel. Two hundred yards beyond, the floor fell out from beneath them again. Eager to escape the entrapping ice, Osaji commanded the ark to begin a descent. A valley opened up before them, and the navigational station that had gone dead months before suddenly came to life. "It's recognized where we are!" Osaji cried out. "We're back in the Saltese Sea!"

The map on the screen showed that they had returned over the mountain range barely twenty miles from the place where they had left it, close to the Cleft of Golconda. No longer were there any boiling plumes; far below them, the familiar currents had resumed. There was even a scattering of dots for the beacons of an arkswarm. Osaji seized the radio and put out a call.

"Any ark, this is *Divernon*. Please respond."

There was silence. She repeated the call.

A crackly, faraway voice came from the speaker. "Which ark is that? Please repeat your call."

"It's *Divernon!*" Osaji nearly shouted.

"*Divernon?*" There was a pause. "Where are you?"

"Above you, just under the ice. We've just come back over the mountains. We were swept across when Golconda erupted, but we made it back."

There were some staticky sounds from the radio that might have been exclamations of surprise, or a conversation on the other end, or merely interference.

"*Divernon*, did you say mountains?" the radio finally said. "We can't have heard you right. Please repeat."

7. Breaking Free

They repeated their story many times in the hours, and finally days, that followed, as they sank back into the inhabited depths and the radio communication improved. They learned that the seafloor station at Golconda had not been utterly destroyed. Though the main dome had collapsed in the earthquake, and the port facilities had been severely damaged, the auxiliary domes had survived, and now the main one was being rebuilt. Through a friend of a friend, Osaji even learned that Kitti and her family were all right.

"She will be very surprised to see her sister again," the woman said over the radio. "The name of Osaji was listed among the casualties."

The paddletails revived as they sank into warmer water, and started towing them upstream again. Since this would take the ark by the fastest route to Golconda, they let them continue. Osaji relished the idea of arriving pulled by a snakeherd in their makeshift harnesses.

As they neared the station, Osaji dutifully started to pack and clean in order to vacate their purloined vessel. She had not entered Mota's vacuole since they had started the journey home. It was just as she had left it. Hardening herself against the memories, Osaji started to fill a recycling bin with the possessions of Mota's lifetime. She was standing with Uncle Yamada's flute in her hand when Jack peered in.

"Do you suppose anyone would value Yamada's flute?" she said.

He came in and took the flute, but gave it back. "Not like you would," he said.

"I can't keep it," she said. "Someone else will use this vac next round. One must clear everything away so the next round can begin." She stuffed the flute in the trash.

"I'll take it, then," Jack said, and fished it out.

"Does it play?" she asked.

He blew over the airhole and it let out a protesting squawk. "I guess I'll have to learn how," he said. "Or Yamada will haunt me."

He looked around the small bubble. "She was a nice lady. Not at all like you." Realizing what he'd said, he winced. "That's not what I meant."

Osaji knew what he'd meant, and didn't mind. She didn't want to be like Mota. At least one person on Ben knew that about her.

"So what's next for you?" he said. "You going to settle down and have a normal life now?"

Osaji felt as if the room were listening for her answer. Claustrophobia suddenly oppressed her. "Let's go outside," she said. "Maybe we can see Golconda now."

All was blackness outside, except the glowing ark itself. They swam around and sat atop it, silent with their crowded thoughts. At last Osaji said, "Do spacers always go back to space?"

"No, I think I'll give Ben another try," he said.

"Good," Osaji answered.

He turned to look at her. Through his facemask, his expression was indistinguishable. "You never answered my question."

Osaji still couldn't answer right away. Even out here, she felt the pull of community and family and duty, tugging at her to become the woman she ought to be.

Then, defying it all, she said, "I want to go over the mountains again."

"Really?" he said.

"Yes. I want to find what else is out there. I want to explore the glass city, and know what happened to its builders."

"Yeah," he said.

"Will Jack go back?"

"I think I may. I've decided you Bennites have something here, with these arks, this autopoiesis thing."

"It's not a new idea," Osaji said. It was, in fact, as old as life.

"No, but it's a better idea than you realize. Permeable membranes, that's the key: a constant exchange between outside and in. You've got to let the world leak in, and let yourself flow out into the nutrient bath around you. You've got to let in ideas, and observations, and … well, affection … or you become hard and dead inside. Life is all about having a permeable self—not so you're unclear who you are, but so you overlap a little with the others on the edges."

Osaji was too surprised to say anything. She could not imagine anyone less permeable than Jack. But as she thought about it, and herself, she said hesitantly, "Some people are too permeable. They spend their lives trying to flow out, and never take in nutrient for themselves. They end up thin and empty inside."

Just then, she saw a mote of light ahead. "Look!" she cried.

It was Golconda. Ahead waited joyous reunions, amazing tales, celebrations of a new future. Once they arrived with their news, the planet would never be the same.

"All the same," Jack said, "I think I'll take an outboard motor next time."

"I —wait," Stu said.

"No time," the man said again. He lifted up the cuff of his left pant leg. A metal band lay atop his ankle. "It's a direction-finder. I've got to get out of here." The bald man stared at him amid the cricket cheeps. "You're a good man, I can tell."

Stu stared back.

"Take care of my daughter," the man said. "And don't ever tell her about this."

The pistol felt like dead weight in Stu's hand. Crooked under his elbow was the box of money.

A reef of clouds drifted away from the moon. Suddenly white light filled the yard, spilling onto the intruder's form. Stu noted the tears streaming down the strange man's face. He also noticed—

Mittens? Stu thought.

The man seemed to be wearing mittens. *Mittens, in summer?*

But that was it.

Stu couldn't think of anything to say as the bald man disappeared across the yard into the darkness.